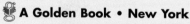

A Golden Book • New York

Back cover photography courtesy of copyright holders:
© Comstock Images
© Royalty Free/CORBIS

Copyright © 2005 by Edith Kunhardt. All rights reserved under International and Pan-American Copyright
Conventions. Published in the United States by Golden Books, an imprint of Random House Children's Books,
a division of Random House, Inc., New York, and simultaneously in Canada by Random House of
Canada Limited, Toronto. Golden Books, A Golden Book, and the G colophon are registered trademarks
of Random House, Inc. pat the bunny® is a registered trademark of PENK, Inc., and Random House, Inc.
PAT THE BUNNY® PLAYDATE BOOKS is a trademark of PENK, Inc., and Random House, Inc.
"pat the..."™ is a trademark of PENK, Inc., and Random House, Inc.
Library of Congress Control Number: 2004112824

www.goldenbooks.com

ISBN: 0-307-10604-7

MANUFACTURED IN SINGAPORE

10 9 8 7 6 5 4 3 2 1

Daddy's Scratchy Face

By Edith Kunhardt

Daddy's face is scratchy.
Itchy scratchy,
when Paul and Judy
kiss Daddy in the morning.
Why is Daddy's face scratchy?
Because hair grows on it.

Is Mummy's face scratchy?

Are Paul's and Judy's
faces scratchy?
No!
Because men grow beards.
Women and children do not.

Daddy shaves his scratchy face.
Then his face is smooth and soft.

The next day, his face is scratchy!
And he has to shave again.

Great-Granddad.

Uncle Charlie.

Great-
Great-
Granddad.

Who else has hair?
Itchy scratchy hair?
Elephants have hair
on their chins and all
over their bodies.

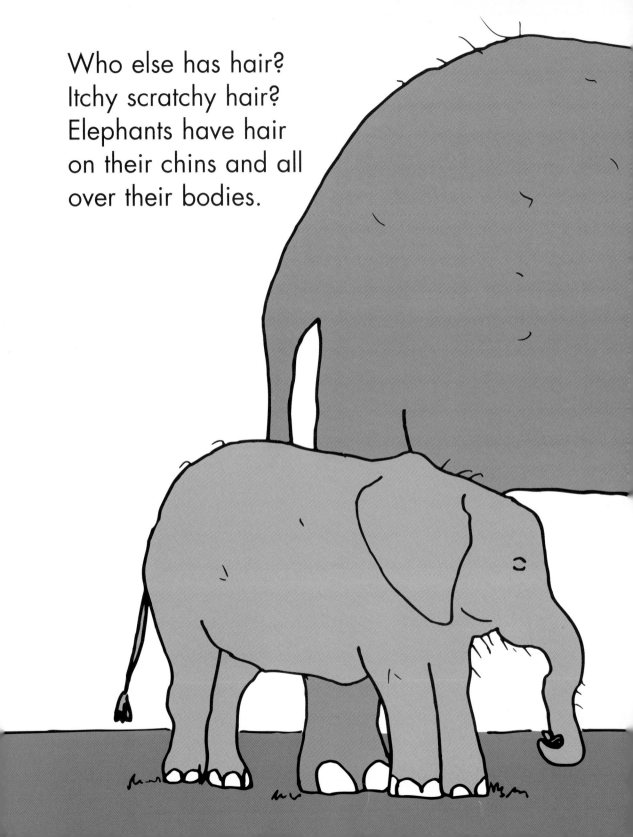

A cat has whiskers
by her soft pink nose.
She can tell with her whiskers
if a space is wide enough
for her to pass through.

A bison has a beard and so does a goat!

Some owls have beards and mustaches made out of feathers.

A catfish's whiskers help it get
around the murky water.

Humpback whales have hairs on their snouts. The hairs help the whales to feel their way through the ocean.

A lion has a beardlike mane that reaches all around his head.

A tiger has a white beard
under his chin.

The beard of an orangutan
is the color of ginger.
Is it itchy? Is it scratchy?
Does the orangutan
shave his beard every day,
just like Daddy?

No!
Animals don't shave.
People shave.
Daddies shave.

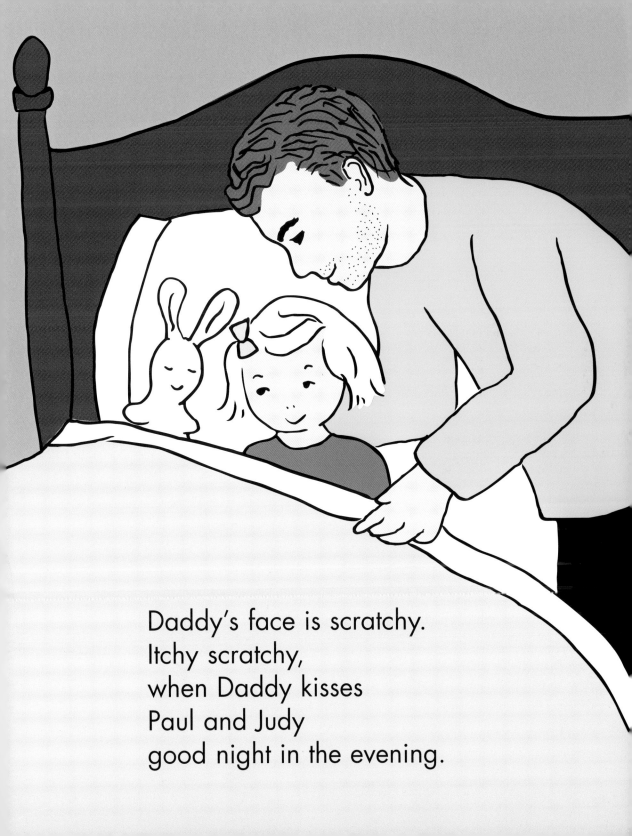

Daddy's face is scratchy.
Itchy scratchy,
when Daddy kisses
Paul and Judy
good night in the evening.

Good night!